T0168466

GOLF IN THE YEAR 2100

GOLF IN THE YEAR 2100

2100

A Fanciful Glimpse at the Future of Golf

Bob Labbance

TowleHouse Publishing
Nashville, Tennessee

TowleHouse books are distributed by National Book Network (NBN),
4720 Boston Way, Lanham, Maryland 20706.

Library of Congress Cataloging-in-Publication Data

Labbance, Bob.
  Golf in the year 2100 : a fanciful glimpse at the future of golf / Bob
Labbance.
     p. cm. -- (Good golf!)
  ISBN 1-931249-23-7 (alk. paper)
  1. Golfers--Fiction. I. Title. II. Series.
  PS3612.A25G65 2003
  813'.6--dc21

                                                          2003007722

Cover design by Gore Studio, Inc.
Page design by Mike Towle

Printed in the United States of America
1 2 3 4 5 6—07 06 05 04 03

To my great kids Griffin and Simone, in hopes they live long enough to see if any of this comes true

ACKNOWLEDGMENTS.

THANKS TO PATRICK WHITE, Rob Halpert, Bunkie Foozle, and all the brilliant people at Notown Communications of Montpelier, Vermont. I don't know how I could have done it without their input, insight, editing, and support. What a terrific company.

Also thanks to Drs. Barry Messinger and Tom Curchin for medical advice; visionaries Brian Tyrol, Bill Amick, and Doug Keffer; writers Brian Siplo, David Cornwell, Kevin Mendik, Tom Bedell, J. Peter Martin, Bill Van Liew, Arthur Ristau, David DeSmith, Ralph Wimbish, Dave Anderson, Herb Wind, Chuck Stogel, Dan Wexler, Tom Mackin, Noel Neff, David Outerbridge, Hal Phillips, Steve Piatt, Tony Pioppi, Pete Georgiady, Alistair

Johnston, Dave Sprague, Bill Noble, and Wayne Mills; friends Scott Peters, Adelaide Murphy, Jon Kostka, Mel Lucas, Jim Hickman, Dr. Margaret Hanni, Ed Homsey, Rees Jones, Geoff Cornish, Roger Rulewich, Marshall Victor, Serena Fox, and Heinz Valenta; associates Paul Sachs, Martin Davis, Mike Towle, Paul Richardson, Steve Smyers, Bud Thompson, Ben Hale, Mike Beckerich, Bob Montgomery, and David Cassidy; all the golf course superintendents who have taken a moment of their time to chat; Bandon Dunes Resort; my dear mother and mother-in-law; and my lovely wife Kathie.

PREFACE.

A LITTLE OVER ONE HUNDRED years ago, horse and buggy was the most rapid mode of personal travel; the telegraph the fastest method of communication; the average life expectancy around forty-eight; and doctors still believed in leeches as a medical practice to purify the blood. The idea of machines flying like birds was the crazy dream of Wilbur and Orville Wright; the best source of information was the encyclopedia at the local library; and many people farmed the land in order to survive.

Golf was played on five-thousand-yard courses with clubs made of wood, balls made of tree sap, and tees made of sand. A long drive traveled two hundred yards, greens rolled at less than half the speed of today, and the next tee was usually two club lengths from the previous hole. It was in this environment that J. McCullough wrote his 1892 book *Golf in the Year 2000,* and predicted television, bullet trains, digital watches, and red golfing jackets that yelled, "Fore" whenever the ball was hit.

With the advances made in the century since McCullough's volume, and the rapid rate of progress and change we take for granted today, who's to say that the brave new world Martin Grant finds himself in at the start of *Golf in the Year 2100* is inaccurate? Like his predecessor in McCullough's book, Grant feels like an alien in his homeland—a place where thoughts are projected, inanimate objects are interactive, and people live 125 years. Grant finds golf to be a comfort—at least until scorecards start talking, the course environment can be altered at whim, combatants try to disable one another on the fairway, and everything from balls, bags, and hazards are suspended in space.

If you'd like to join him, open your mind, put aside your reliance on today's conventions, and hop on board. The next hovercraft leaves in a moment.

CHAPTER I.

In 2003.

IT HAD BEEN ONE of those perfect days—the kind that come around once or twice a golfing season. The type you put in your memory banks to draw on when you're out on the course and it's raining, your partners are crabby, and you have absolutely no swing.

The temperature was hovering around eighty degrees, the southerly breeze was light, the air was clear, and the sun was setting over the Pacific in a blaze of lavender and hot pink. We played the back nine at Pebble Beach in the twilight, and by the end we felt like we were the only ones on the course. I had a good round going—tagging my driver 275 down the middle with regularity, hitting crisp approach shots, and chipping and putting as if I knew what I was doing. I came to the eighteenth needing a par to shoot 78, which would be my best score ever at this holy shrine of golf.

1

At the last I cracked a drive that hugged the coastline and left me only 240 to the flag. Might as well go for it, I reasoned, you only live once. Took out the four-wood, told myself to swing easy, and, of course, lashed at it with all my might like most eleven-handicappers. But instead of yanking it into the ocean, which I have been known to do, I sailed the ball straight toward the green's entryway, and it pulled up just short of the putting surface. I licked my chops as I removed the eight-iron from the bag and prepared for a pitch and run to the back flag-stick position. *Don't chili-dip it,* I thought. *Just get it close and you might even have a chance at birdie.*

Despite having a career round at hand, like most amateurs I allowed my mind to wander as I approached the ball. I thought of how lucky we all were to be standing near the eighteenth green at Pebble Beach and how stunning the surroundings would have appeared to someone who had never experienced them before. I then backed away and tried to refocus. I was determined to put a good pitch-and-run stroke on the ball.

I hit the tiny spot I had picked out just a few paces onto the putting surface and the ball headed toward the back of the green. When that runner clinked against the middle of the flagstick and dove into the bottom of the hole there was a whoop from my playing partners; eagle threes are not a common score in our circle, and 76 at Pebble was unheard of, at least in our group. I couldn't have been in a better mood as we adjourned to the watering hole— even treating my buddies to a couple of rounds of grog at the Lodge.

As I motored along Seventeen-Mile Drive on the way home, I replayed several of the holes in my mind, savoring the pleasure. I couldn't wait to share the high with my fifteen-year-old son, himself an up-and-coming high school player of local renown. As I rounded the turn just past the Carmel Gate, reality struck hard. A delivery truck, out of control, was over in my lane and bearing down on me rapidly. A wall hugged the right side of the road and there was no bailout. My evasive reaction was swift but fruitless. The last thing I remember was the sight of the scorecard flying out of the visor and heading toward the floor. Everything after that was a blank.

Chapter II.

THE FIRST THING I remember is what felt like a single pinprick in the big toe on my left foot. I was annoyed that someone would be piercing my skin, but the thought was fleeting as I quickly fell back under the spell of a deep slumber.

When I reached the surface of consciousness again it felt as if there were many pinpricks—that tingling sensation you get when your foot falls asleep—and I tried to shake my leg to "wake it up," only to drift off again without ever opening my eyes.

The next episode was more of a jolt. I felt a pain akin to a stabbing rather than a prick, and it was enough to get my attention—even yanking me out of the delicious golfing dream in which my subconscious had been embroiled. My eyelids retracted like a rusty old garden gate. As my eyes struggled to focus, I could see several people standing around peering at me.

"He's opened his eyes; he's coming to," someone said. Suddenly, there was a flurry of activity from across the room.

"Can you hear us?" someone in a lab coat asked as he advanced toward me.

"Yes," I croaked in a voice that clearly hadn't had much practice of late. "Where am I?"

"You're at Western Wellness," offered a giant of a man, "and I'm Dr. Stillwater. Welcome back to planet Earth."

Humor was yet beyond my capacities.

"What planet have I been on?" I countered.

"I'm afraid that's a long story," Stillwater chuckled. "We'll address all your questions when you're more able to assimilate the answers. Just try to relax for a moment while we run some additional tests."

Stillwater waved what looked like a magic wand across my torso, while lights flashed and tones sounded at a bank of machines across the room. I'd been in a few hospitals in my forty-nine years, but none of them looked much like this. Slowly, my eyes were starting to focus on the people, the equipment, and the environment around me—everything looked bizarre.

Stillwater was back. "Your name is Martin Grant, is it not?" he queried.

"That's correct," I said, finding my voice a little stronger than it had been moments before.

"And are you an ornithologist?" Stillwater continued.

I hesitated, as the synapses took a little longer to fire than I was accustomed to.

"No, why do you ask?"

"For the last week, as we slowly brought you back to consciousness, the only word out of you was *eagle*, which seemed a likely clue as to your profession."

Though I still wasn't positive what I could and couldn't do, that statement made me realize I still had the ability to smile. "No, I'm an attorney. The eagle I was referring to was the one I made on the eighteenth hole at Pebble Beach, just before my car was hit by a truck on Seventeen-Mile Drive." The pleasurable feeling of that glorious day was washing over me once again, but with it came the concern for the rest of my golfing buddies and for my family. Why weren't they bedside, thrilled I was regaining consciousness?

Stillwater was amused. "Ah, a fellow golfer," he beamed. "We'll have much to talk about. I've heard great things about Pebble Beach. What a terrific course it must have been."

No family? No more Pebble Beach? What was going on? As the questions raced through my brain I started to drift away again. The last thing I heard was someone saying, "We're losing him . . ."

WHEN I WOKE UP again, I found myself seated in a chair. Stillwater entered the room, and as he strode toward me I realized once again how big he really was. He must have stood over seven feet tall.

"Feeling better?" he asked. I had to admit I did, as if more cobwebs had been brushed away and I was finally processing information correctly. "We had one more blood vessel to attach to the motor section of your brain; it had escaped us in previous scans. Your capacities should be just about back to normal now."

I felt around my head. No signs of an incision or operation. My questions were mounting.

"Mr. Grant, do you have any idea what has happened to you?" the doctor asked.

"Did I fall into a coma after the accident, and am just coming out of it?"

This seemed a logical conclusion on my part, but I had to admit it didn't address all the discrepancies my brain was picking up on.

"A good guess for a man of your era, but there's actually a great deal more to it than that. Are you prepared to hear the whole story?"

I had already dismissed the fact I might be having a dream, or that an elaborate hoax was being perpetrated by some of my pals. There just didn't seem to be a case for that. And since I found little other evidence that seemed logical or believable, I put myself in the hands of the doctor.

"I'm ready," I uttered.

"Mr. Grant, the accident you had on the road leaving Pebble Beach nearly killed you. When you arrived at the hospital that day, your right lung was collapsed, your liver was punctured, your spinal cord was severely damaged, and you had multiple fractures of your left leg, pelvis, and rib cage. You had little pulse, less brain function, and little chance for survival. Face it, you were in a bad way."

Although this was not surprising given my vague memories of the moments before the crash, it was shocking considering those issues no longer seemed to be problems. "So why am I sitting here talking to you, seemingly in one piece?"

"From what we can tell, you received excellent emergency care at the hospital. However, when it appeared doctors would be unable to do anything about your liver or brain injuries, your family produced a legal document that you had drawn up calling for your body to be cryogenically frozen in the event of life-threatening injuries that might be correctable in the future. You were put in a state of suspended animation, moved to inland California, and placed in a facility designed to store and eventually revive people in your circumstances. This was not unheard of in that era."

Even though there were now more questions than answers, I let Stillwater continue.

"In 2042, the massive earthquake everyone had feared for decades finally hit. Much of the West Coast, including Pebble Beach and all of the Monterey Peninsula, fell into the Pacific. The cryogenic lab you were stored in was buried under seventy-five feet of rocks and mud, and the company that ran the lab feared everyone was lost."

My head, which had been feeling fine, was now starting to spin. I was speechless and couldn't even imagine what was next. "It wasn't until a second major earthquake hit this year, that your containment cylinder was jarred loose and forced back up to the surface," the doctor continued. "Amazingly, the hydrogen cell that had powered your refrigeration was still functioning. Even though the technology for tissue cryogenics has been outdated for decades, we were able to bring you back to life and correct your injuries by consulting obsolete scientific methodology. You are as healthy as the day you made that eagle on eighteen."

Like the first generation of personal computers, my brain was processing the information that was being inputted, but it would be a while before assimilation was complete. I blinked; I gulped; I breathed deeply; my brain formed 218 questions that battled with each other to reach my mouth. But all that came out was: "What day is it?"

"Today is July 7, 2100," pronounced Stillwater. "Welcome to the twenty-second century."

10

Chapter III.

PLANETARY INFORMATION NETWORK—HOVERCRAFT
TECHNOLOGY—FLOATING HOUSE—ARTIFICIAL
INTELLIGENCE—A VISIT, OF SORTS, TO ST. ANDREWS.

STILLWATER LEFT ME ALONE to absorb that bomb-shell; meanwhile, his staff had prepared a brief-ing paper that outlined world history over the past century. It was hard to concentrate on the words. Thoughts of my personal situation kept taking precedence: What had become of my family? Had my residence disappeared into the Pacific in what must have been the ultimate natural disaster? Why do I feel so good after life-threatening injuries and one hundred years of slumber? Are there others in my situation? What happens next?

I must have drifted off again, because when my eyes reopened, the doctor was once again standing before me. "So, I'm sure you're wondering what's next, Mr. Grant," Stillwater offered, as if he had been reading my mind. "There's really no further need for you to remain here, as you are physically well and completely able to travel. We have not submitted your story to the Planetary Information Network as we did not want to invade your privacy, and we're still in the dark regarding how to find your next of kin. I would be happy to host you in my residence, where you would have all the time you need to sort this out and plan your next move. Maybe we could even enjoy a round of golf together to help you gain perspective."

With few other options presenting themselves and a 150-year-old brain already in overload, I accepted the doctor's offer. The familiarity of golf offered some comfort and, in fact, sounded pretty damn inviting at this point. Everything else seemed alien.

"I don't know how to prepare you for what the outside looks like," Stillwater offered. "We're charting new patient-care territory for me." He laughed. "I live about a hundred miles from here, but we'll be there in ten to fifteen minutes—depending on traffic, of course." That made it sound like one of California's biggest problems of the twentieth century had been solved. In my commuting experience, a hundred miles could have easily taken three hours.

During the trip to the Stillwater residence, I was aware that my mouth was open, a blank stare on my face; I also realized it wasn't going to be a one-time occurrence. For starters, Western Wellness wasn't a hospital—I was later told there were no more hospitals—it was a city. The multibuilding complex included a giant dome, a centrally located park, and a supporting infrastructure that defied my knowledge. And we didn't get into a car to make the trip; we used the doc's hovercraft.

The transporter looked like a small, comfortable room with space for two passengers. Stillwater programmed a flight plan into an onboard monitor and waited for clearance, which came almost instantly. As we rose nearly vertically I could see streams of the crafts at various levels. "I know they experimented with hovercraft technology back in your day, Mr. Grant, but it wasn't until the 2050s that it was perfected. The initial conversion was problematic, especially in urban areas, but the system operates smoothly these days. Slower local traffic moves along the old roadways just as it did for you, but the atmosphere is divided into stratas, and the farther and faster you want to go, the higher your assigned travel range. Once we climb this ascension column, we'll be two thousand feet up, traveling at six hundred miles per hour. Enjoy the ride."

I tried to act casual and enjoy the trip; after all, I'd been in many small private planes in my day, and this flight's sensation wasn't all that much different. It just looked bizarre to see thousands of these George Jetson-type craft streaming along in the air. "I'm surprised we can't just beam over there, like they did in *Star Trek*," I offered nervously. The doctor had obviously seen the show, which in itself was quite remarkable. "That technology does exist," Stillwater countered. "But so far scientists have only been successful with inanimate objects. We can send an apple anywhere we want, but humans are more problematic. Organs kept getting left behind, and reassembling people is time consuming. Possible . . . but time consuming."

MY TIME AT THE doctor's home was akin to college
. . . make that elementary school. Everything was a
new experience with no basis in my previous experience on the planet. For one thing, the house was
not connected to the ground. Rather, it "floated"
several stories above two other domiciles that were
also stacked above ground level. This mitigated
damage from future earthquakes and allowed for a
marvelous view of the California coastline in the
distance, just as if we were perched on a large hill
with 360-degree views. Judging from earthbound
abodes I had seen on the trip, the doctor lived in
one of Mendocino's better neighborhoods.

The home featured an invisible umbrella that
protected it from the elements. Giant fans kept the
air moving even when the coastal fog rolled in. The
interior walls changed daily. When we first arrived,
Stillwater had them set to off-white with no adorn-
ments. A few days later they displayed a rain forest
scene; later they became a museum with some of
the world's greatest artwork. Once personal prefer-
ences were logged, rooms could change to suit the
desires of the person entering. Stillwater demon-
strated one of his favorites: tapestries from a temple

in northern India. They were so lifelike it wasn't until you were inches away that you realized they were only a projection.

Food tasted similar to what I knew, but looked entirely different. After a few days of eating fresh vegetables, Stillwater informed me about what a delicacy they were. "The only fresh food is grown on the moon," he said. "There is not enough clean air or fresh water in any outdoor environment on Earth to grow commercial quantities of food; and there's no space for a large enough indoor facility. Small farms completely disappeared decades ago, and most of the large-scale operations depleted the soil so thoroughly it took years to reconstruct." The processed food was highly concentrated— "power flavor" Stillwater called it. Tiny portions were cut up, and once inside your mouth they combined with saliva to expand in both volume and taste. Further expansion occurred during digestion, giving diners the feeling of filling up but without the bulk. If science hadn't stepped in with this advancement, millions of people would have starved as populations outgrew the limited capacity of food purveyors.

CHAPTER III.

I spent a week learning about the past century, the current world order, and advances in many fields of human endeavor. To my surprise there were still books to learn from. Even in the midst of strange surroundings that had no basis in my experience, I found books a profound comfort. I read voraciously, keeping a dictionary at my side. I imagined how inadequate someone from 1900 would have felt confronting the jargon of 2000, and realized how many words we coin in the course of a decade, let alone a century. Medical and informational technologies were the two areas that most boggled my mind.

Even in the midst of strange surroundings that had no basis in my experience, I found books a profound comfort. I read voraciously, keeping a dictionary at my side.

Given my twentieth-century mentality, I expected to find computers everywhere. Instead, they were nonexistent—at least that's how it seemed at first glance. "Computers as you know them disappeared nearly seventy-five years ago," Stillwater noted. "Instead, computer *chips* are part of everything. Computer circuitry can be woven into microthin fibers; even liquids can be imbued with computation characteristics. Artificial intelligence is in clothing, appliances, equipment—even you."

He could tell I was puzzled by that. "You were chipped the moment we brought you to Western Wellness. In a hospital from your era, you would have been hooked up to monitors and banks of diagnostic equipment. As you noticed, we no longer have those systems. At birth, a tiny chip is inserted in most people that monitors all body functions—heart rate, blood pressure, cholesterol, red blood-cell count, vitamin or mineral deficiency, cancer cell development, gene mutation . . . everything. That information is transmitted to a home monitor, and, in times of disease or crisis, the information can be transmitted and interpreted by a center such as Western Wellness. There is far more to it than that, but we don't need to go into all the details yet."

"Where is the information projected?" I queried. "I haven't seen a computer screen yet."

"When force-field technology (FFT) was perfected, the need for projection monitors was over," Stillwater said. "Air particles can be assembled in any order and used in a myriad of applications, including the ability to display images. Hence, information can be shown anywhere in space, but most surprisingly, also on the cornea of your eye, giving you a private showing, per se. I can introduce you to that in a way that I know you'll enjoy. How about a round of simulated golf?"

IN AGREEING TO THE experiment, I pictured the early efforts of simulation science from the century with which I was familiar. People were hooked up to electrodes at multiple points on their bodies and bulky eyepieces were fastened to their head. By the time all the gear was installed, it felt like I was playing golf in a suit of armor—and smooth, tension-free swings were as common as blue moons in July.

For the 2100 version, the doctor informed me that all I needed was a chip upgrade. "Does that involve an operation?" I naively inquired.

"No, it doesn't," Stillwater answered with a smirk. "There is infinite versatility built into the chip we already installed in you. I hesitated to engage the corneal projection mechanism until I had briefed you. The first few experiences can be rather dizzying. Are you ready for me to adjust your field of vision?"

As I gave the go-ahead, Stillwater fiddled with what looked like a television remote control.

Within seconds, printing scrolled through my field of view. I was reading a welcome message from St. Andrews in Scotland, which briefed me on today's course conditions and asked me if I was ready to play. "What about clubs?" I asked.

"You don't need them," my host said. "Just think what you need to have in your hand, based on the yardage projection, and you'll have it. When you're ready to begin, just inform your mind, and you'll be good to go."

The thought crossed my mind, and a second later I was standing on the first tee at the Home of Golf. My entire field of view was the Auld Grey Town and the linksland that supported the course. For all practical purposes, I was no longer in Stillwater's home— at least not according to my overtaxed cerebral cortex. "What if I've had enough?" I asked in a panic— and instantly I was back in the doc's living room. "It's that easy," he chuckled, "but you'll miss your tee time standing here."

I gave in to the feeling again. The next thing I knew I had killed a drive three hundred yards down the first fairway. I was hooked. Over the next hour I was almost convinced I was at St. Andrews. I could see the ball at my feet, feel the breeze on my face, taste the salty air blowing off the water, and smell the freshly mown turf. And just by thinking *four-iron* it was in my hand and ready for my next swing.

If anyone has ever been in need of a good excuse for not playing well, I was that person. Remember, I hadn't hit a club in almost a century. There had to be a little rust. Ninety-seven years! As it turned out, my score was well above my usual game, though I did seem to hit the ball an awfully long way.

When I holed out at eighteen, I thought *home* and there I was, back in the living room, a grinning doctor standing next to me. "That was incredible!" I exclaimed.

"That was nothing," Stillwater said. "I think you're ready for some real golf, and I have some time tomorrow. I thought we'd start out with a traditional course."

"As opposed to what?"

"Well, X-Golf is wildly popular these days, especially among the younger players. But that might be a little too fringe for your mental state at the moment. Let's take it one step at a time."

"I'm ready," I said—only half believing it.

CHAPTER IV.

STILLWATER HAD CHOSEN THE Bandon Dunes complex in Oregon for our first golf outing. He wanted a spectacular venue for our round, and, as he had explained, the courses of the Monterey Peninsula had all fallen into the Pacific Ocean in the massive earthquake of 2042. "Besides, they're building a seventh course at Bandon," he added. "Course construction is so radically different than a hundred years ago, you really should see it."

Since its founding, Bandon had long been one of the beacons for golf traditionalists in America. Though their recently opened layouts had kept pace with the new science of golf, they remained one of those rare North America spots still true to golf's ancient ideals. Many players came solely for that connection.

Before we traveled the several hundred miles to Bandon, we headed off to the shopping district so I could get ahold of some equipment. Although most anything could be obtained from one's residence, the doctor thought I would benefit from a proper fitting. "I don't know if I have anything in a traditional set for someone of such small stature," the clerk said in a condescending manner. "I'll check the inventory."

Although I hadn't been out in public much yet, I realized that my five-foot-nine frame, somewhat average for my era, was rather small in the 2100 world. My host towered at least a foot over me. I asked him about average heights.

"Two hundred years ago, five feet, six inches was tall," Stillwater explained. "Today people often attain seven feet in height, with professional athletes growing to eight feet and even a little beyond. It's just the natural progression of the human species.

"Likewise, our life expectancy has increased proportionally. In 1900 the average male lived to be forty-eight; in 2000 it was closer to seventy-three; today it's ninety-five. With the medical science we have at our disposal, there are many people who live to be 125 or more."

I felt young again.

The clerk reappeared with a set of golf sticks. On the surface they looked much the same as the ones I had played with at Pebble Beach during my last round—that is, until I touched them. The clubs were amazingly light, especially for the strength and mass of the clubheads. The shaft cut through the air like butter, though they barely bent when I applied pressure to the standing stick. The heads were thinner and smaller than I was used to, and they were constructed from an unadorned black metal that had a textured finish. There were no grooves. "You can adjust the amount of texture to the clubface with this dial," Stillwater said as I looked askance. "And it's legal."

I was most surprised by the driver the clerk produced—it was made of wood—and I was just about to express this to my host. "The wood has been genetically altered," the doctor said, noticing my surprise. "It has been cultivated specifically for golf clubs and offers more strength than any metal. Yet it retains a soft feel. Talented players can power the ball amazing distances. Furthermore, the sensitivity of the wood facilitates manipulating the ball any way you choose. High cuts, low hooks, or frozen rope line drives are all easier with Genwood11J2 than with metallic composites. You'll get the feel at the range before we tee it up."

"Could you please send them on to Bandon Dunes?" the doctor asked the store clerk. Having no currency, and not yet having seen any exchanged, I was concerned about payment; never mind my concern regarding whether my clubs would reach our destination in time.

"Everything's taken care of," Stillwater said, sensing my unease as we exited. "The clubs will be Teletransported to the site—they're probably there by now. And payment is through the Global Depository. All private and national banks merged many years ago. When you enter any commercial establishment, sensors take a retina print—no two human eyes are alike—and the amount is automatically deducted from your master account. The system has made cash, checks, and credit cards virtually

"When you enter any commercial establishment, sensors take a retina print—no two human eyes are alike—and the amount is automatically deducted from your master account."

obsolete." I was beginning to accept these advance-
ments as routine, but I have to admit I was still mysti-
fied how my host constantly knew what my next question would be. Was he just an intuitive man or were
other forces at work here? I decided not to confront
that one at this time.

Our ride to Oregon was quick and uneventful,
though we needed to discuss what we would tell our
playing partners about my story. "Even though it
might put you in some odd positions, I don't think
we should 'break cover' with your account just yet,"
Stillwater said. "Let's just say you've been away from
golf for several decades and are taking it up again."
I accepted that approach, but I also realized I had to
be on guard—it's easy to look like a fool when
you've been out of circulation for a century.

In one way I already felt like an imposter.
Simple hospital garb was acceptable for lounging
around Stillwater's residence; going to play golf was
another matter. Just as the red golfing coat, plus-
fours, patterned socks, white shirt, and skinny
necktie had been de rigueur in the 1890s, looking
good in 2100 meant conforming to what the other
players wore. Showing up in year 2000 garb—

logoed golf shirt, comfortable sweater vest, and cotton slacks—would have looked just as outdated as wearing plus-fours would have looked in the era I had exited.

As far as I could tell, people wore a single layer of covering most of the time—a layer so thin it was hard to think of it as clothing. Stillwater had already explained to me that the membrane created a body habitat, one molecule in thickness, within which a form of air conditioning or heating was activated. Monitors in the fabric calculated the exterior temperature and compared that with your personal comfort zone, then initiated a chemical reaction that created a supercharged cushion of air suited to conditions. Different parts of the body could be treated differently and conditions were evaluated and altered perpetually. The exterior appearance could be changed at will by your emotions, giving new meaning to the old phrase about "wearing your heart on your sleeve."

We were greeted at Bandon by course master Emil Kant, who was waiting in a golf cart hovercraft—Stillwater had called ahead to ask for a tour of the course construction. "As you can see, we're employing the latest magnetic resonance construction techniques," Kant said as we flew across the ocean-side landscape. "Using a hand-held envisioning device, the architect has charted each green, hazard, mound, and depression down to a sixteenth of an inch. When she has every contour on the hole exactly the way she wants it, a magnetic charge will permeate the ground, infiltrating every rock, plant, and soil type designated for removal. A giant magnet will then delete the superfluous material, leaving the exact contours of every feature, just as the architect has planned it. We then spray the rubberized skin atop that. When that sets, we're ready to install the subsurface engineering."

I marveled at how this alien technique would be just as shocking to the twentieth-century course builders and their massive earth-moving equipment as it would have been to Donald Ross with his drag pans and workhorses. But I had to keep my comments to myself as we moved to a hole where the next step was underway.

"Those massive sponges you see attract water molecules through ionization charges, so any natural rainfall or excess irrigation is brought through the soil profile to the collection basins," Kant noted. "It is released from the catch areas when they reach a specific saturation, cleansed, and then fed back into the irrigation system. This recycling is, of course, mandated by federal law. Any overflow is stored in underground chambers for future use."

As an aside, Stillwater informed me that air-borne irrigation also had been outlawed decades ago. As water became a precious resource, any nonnatural public display of it was outlawed. There were no more gushing fountains in front of tall buildings, decorative waterways to frame monuments, or giant plumes of water arching over agricultural fields. Studies had shown that as much as 3 percent of airborne water was lost to evaporation, and that portion was desperately needed. Desalination facilities had helped to augment reserves temporarily—until the level of the planet's oceans started to drop—and then projects of that nature were also subject to scrutiny by the Planetary Resource Monitoring Board (PRMB). Plant-specific underground delivery systems were the only methods approved for usage by the PRMB, and every ounce of water was accounted for in regular water inventory control.

Not only do plants send out an enzyme that alerts the network to water needs, but fertilization, frost protectant, and all known turf diseases are preprogrammed.

"Next comes the irrigation lattice, a web of capillary tubing that can reach every inch of the property," Kant continued. "It is installed several inches below the root structure of the grass plant, and we're using the most sophisticated trigger system ever developed. Not only do plants send out an enzyme that alerts the network to water needs, but fertilization, frost protectant, and all known turf diseases are preprogrammed. If a plant needs help of any kind, all it has to do is alert the central system and the proper control agents will be delivered to the precise area that is calling for it. There's no waste of water or chemicals."

Kant next showed us a hole with the six-inch sand and soil layer installed above the irrigation grid, just as the hydroseeding was to begin. "The top half-inch is a rubberized gypsum containing pre-germinated turfgrass seed, time release fertilizers, and a vegetable paste that glues the stew to the base material. That turf is growing within minutes of application, with wall-to-wall coverage of the acreage within a couple of days. In two weeks, this course will be ready for play."

We slowed to a stop near a tee complex. "Thought you'd be interested in the force-field technology they're installing below the tee box," Kant said. A gauzelike liner was being laid beneath the turf layer, and Stillwater informed me of its function as Kant conferred with a construction superintendent. "Wooden tees are no longer needed to perch your ball above the playing surface," Stillwater noted. "You preset how high in the air you want your ball teed. Then, when you approach the tee, you just place your ball near the ground and the force-field air cushion supports it until you launch your drive."

Once again, I could feel my jaw moving into that perpetually slacked position, especially with our host rejoining us. "Check out the fifth fairway," Kant said as he pointed westward. "They're mowing it for the first time."

Expecting a familiar mowing machine, I had to look closely to see anything different about the adjacent fairway. Eventually, I spotted two tiny hover devices, one on each side of the fairway, precisely following the contours of the light rough. Bridging the gap between them was a beam of light, just above the ground surface. "The lasers work in tandem, progressing from tee to green, and their cut height can be adjusted to the thousandth of an inch. They mow a five-hundred-yard fairway in about five minutes."

I was reeling as Kant left us at the driving range, our clubs waiting in a device that looked like a giant donut. "I assume you want to walk," the doctor said, "although we can take a hover cart if you want to." I assured him that walking was my preference, and he gave me a briefing on my club carrier. The donut would keep my clubs suspended in the air just behind me. It would also tip the bag at the right angle to pull a club when I stopped near my ball and then find the next tee once I pulled my putter for the green. Greenkeepers surely must have been pleased by the elimination of compaction once hover technology was perfected.

The driving range featured a series of greens in the distance. All appeared as if they were hovering in place, with a dark abyss below them. "It's really an illusion," Stillwater said, sensing my confusion over the visual display of the practice area. He certainly had a knack for knowing what I was thinking. "It allows you to focus on hitting a target, with the misdirected shots falling to an irrelevant finish." I didn't even try to comprehend that statement in light of everything else that had gone on already. I just accepted it and stretched a bit before addressing the ball.

My first swipe from the practice ground was a half swing with a lofted club, the kind of pass at the ball that would have propelled it seventy-five yards the last time I played. Instead, the ball rocketed off the clubface and into the endless blue sky. I lost track of it past the 150 marker; Stillwater just laughed. "Feel a little different?" he joked.

I was equally stunned with the six-iron and four-wood—they traveled nearly twice the distance I was accustomed to. Then I picked up the driver. "How far is this going to go?" I asked my host. "You should be able to get 400 to 450 yards out of it," Stillwater countered, "if you keep your head down and swing easy, that is." This indication that the same old tenets still applied was reassuring—at least technology hadn't usurped all the challenge

The donut would keep my clubs suspended in the air just behind me. It would also tip the bag at the right angle to pull a club when I stopped near my ball. (Martin Grant illustration)

from the old game. I wondered how courses still protected par—a concern I would soon realize was quite unnecessary.

I was in a daze as I blasted some moonshots to the far reaches of the driving range, wondering how people followed their balls when they went so far. I was just about to verbalize that question when Stillwater noted that our playing partners had arrived and we were up on the first tee. It seemed that my golf bag sensed this—it was already headed there.

I shook hands with two more giants at the teeing ground. Suddenly, I experienced a slight feeling of familiarity and comfort. We joked about the beautiful conditions, discounted our talents, laid some excuse groundwork for possible poor play, and tried to work out a betting game suitable for all. For a brief moment—if you looked past the odd clothing, the strange nature of the golf clubs, and things hovering everywhere—this was a comfortable place to be. I had stood on the first tee with my buddies hundreds of times in those luscious moments before you've hit a single bad shot, when the day is filled with promise and the camaraderie of a golf round with friends is about to begin. I tried to block out the alien feelings and concentrate on what hadn't changed in a hundred years. A brilliant ocean view was painted over my left shoulder, miles of emerald green fairways stretched out before me, and the sunshine mixed with a stiff and constant wind caressing my face. This is why we play this wonderful game, and I was soaking it in like I hadn't in a long time.

My reverie was broken by the doctor handing me my scorecard, a single piece of plasticized cardboard, which, before I could turn it over to examine the layout, promptly blurted out, "Welcome to Bandon Dunes, Mr. Grant. Can I show you the first hole?"

CHAPTER V.

A FACE IN THE WINDOW—ORDER OF WORLD GOLF—AERIAL HAZARDS—TALKING SCORECARDS—TEEING IT UP WITH THE DOC—RETIRING TO THE GRILL ROOM.

I T'S REALLY HARD TO maintain your composure when the unexpected happens. And although we had good reason to keep my "condition" private for a while longer—and I certainly knew enough already to be expecting some surprises—when your scorecard starts talking to you it's difficult to be casual.

"Or would you rather log in your presets?" the scorecard continued. Sensing my bewilderment, Stillwater whispered, "The scorecard is a sophisticated interactive tool while out on the course. Just follow its lead and you'll be fine."

In glancing back at the card, I noticed that a face had appeared in the window. Like an old friend, it continued to address my needs. We set the height at which I wanted my ball to hover on most tees

(easily overridden for the par-threes or unusual circumstances); activated the ball locator (every golf
ball made had a homing chip built in, so that by
pressing a button on the card, the ball would emit a
signal that prevented lost balls from ruining your
day); entered my handicap (making match-play
games easier to keep track of); and programmed the
level of assistance I required (playing tips for each
hole were standard, but swing analysis and advanced
strategies depending on the wager and talent level
of the player were also available). I chose not to
have a professional examine my swing during the
round, but simply by placing the card on the ground
six inches from the point of impact, the device
could output swing speed, swing plane, clubhead
velocity, and angle of attack—then crunch the
numbers and offer suggestions based on body type,
height, weight, age, and athletic ability. All this
from a three-by-five-inch piece of plastic.

We were playing one of the older courses at
Bandon, but one that had been remodeled in the
past decade. It taped at only 9,384 yards—short by
modern standards, but long when the wind was
howling as it did on many days. The opening hole

The device could output swing speed, swing plane, clubhead velocity, and angle of attack—then crunch the numbers and offer suggestions based on body type, height, weight, age, and athletic ability. (Martin Grant illustration)

was a 522-yard par-four. The four of us were all about the same skill level, although I made it clear to the others that it had been quite a while since I had played golf. They offered me the honor of the tee, and, I have to admit, my knees were knocking as I stepped up. But I made a good pass at the ball and it took off like a rocket.

"Why the nervousness?" asked my scorecard as we walked away from the tee after all had hit. "Your heart rate is nearly twice its normal speed."

I felt odd speaking to a piece of cardboard, and the last thing I needed was unsolicited advice from an inanimate object. "Just first-tee jitters," I muttered, realizing that the card obviously could tune into the information my implanted medical chip outputted. I worried that it might also have built-in lie-detection circuitry. But I couldn't rationalize how that would ever have a positive effect on the golf game. That's why I hoped good reason had prevailed when the technology was available.

"Well, you hit it 346 yards, so relax," came the response. I still wished I could turn the damn thing off.

As we all walked down the opening fairway, our hover bags trailing behind us, I reflected that even though the environment we traversed looked oddly familiar, little about golf was the same as in my former era. As Stillwater had said on the day I awoke, electronics had infiltrated every facet of society. Sophisticated computers were in scorecards, belt buckles, teeing grounds, and golf balls—and, I guessed, in places I couldn't yet imagine.

The interior circuitry of the ball not only allowed it to be found when lost, but also redirected when sprayed. When side-motion spin was above control limits, micro-thrusters inside the ball activated, returning the ball to a straighter flight path. Additional material sensitivity permitted the ball's cover to change on demand. Like a wetting agent, the skin could be made slippery for flight on long shots, sticky for delicate pitches to ultrarapid greens. Some balls even came with explosive charges that were detonated upon contact with the club, but those had yet to be approved by the Order of World Golf (OWG) and are a whole 'nother story.

Based on what it had observed at the practice range, the scorecard recommended a nine-iron for the 176 yards I had left to the flagstick. I took its advice. But I pured the thing and watched it sail over the back of the green and into the tall grass. "You'll have trouble from there," the doctor said as we approached the putting surface. "The green stimps around seventeen today, and it's facing away from you."

Sure enough, despite my best efforts, I found myself back in the fairway after my chip scampered across the putting surface and stopped twenty yards in front of the green. I eventually holed out after four more attempts to come to terms with greens faster than anything I had ever experienced.

As I advanced toward the hole to retrieve my ball, Stillwater motioned me away. "The ball only comes to rest in the hole for a moment before it is whisked away via an underground vacuum system. It's cleaned enroute and appears on the next tee, already hovering at the correct height. It's called the Keffetube—invented by a guy who hated bending over to pick his ball out of the hole. Quite a popular innovation as the population got wider," the doctor laughed. The rest of the foursome had fewer problems with the putting green, with two pars and a bogey being tallied before we moved to the second.

"The second hole is a 790-yard, double dog-leg par-five," the scorecard announced. "Be careful of the aerial hazard 250 out."

I saw the massive solitary tree on the first corner and assumed that was the hazard referred to, so I set my targets left of the limbs and made another nice swing. As the ball flew away, I noticed that a strange-looking and low-flying cloud had now appeared in its flight path, hovering forty yards above the fairway about 250 yards away. My ball entered the cloud and instantly dropped down to the ground just off the fairway. The results seemed to defy all the laws of gravity I could remember, but I tried to take it in stride.

Stillwater took me aside once again as we walked off the tee. "I didn't want to tell you about aerial hazards until I needed to," he said, sounding like a consoling father. "Long ago, force-field technology permitted any collection of air molecules to be imbued with mass and volume. The cloud you hit into is actually a field of heavy air that's about the same as hitting your ball into Jell-O. As soon as it entered the hazard, the ball was derailed toward the ground. Aerial challenges of this nature were approved for play by the OWG decades ago. The course can arrange them differently every day—it's one tool employed to protect par and keep the longer hitters from bombing the ball 450 yards. I didn't want to fill you in because it's just like the unseen water hazard. As soon as you point it out to a golfer, the chances of him hitting it into the water increases substantially. I don't want to predispose you to any bad fortune."

I thanked the doctor and gazed skyward as we approached my ball. The cloud looked just like any other, and I noted several others hovering out in front of me over the remaining five hundred yards of the hole. One such cloud, however, was positioned directly between me and the putting surface, preventing me from a full shot aimed at the green. So I laid up with a three-hundred-yard four-iron.

I was comforted by the fact that one of the experienced players accompanying me failed to negotiate an aerial hazard, as his ball was forced down into the deep rough halfway to the hole. "At least they're stable today," Stillwater noted. "Some days the aerials are in constant motion, and that makes avoiding them even trickier."

CHAPTER V.

I managed a bogey on the par-five. Since no one made par, I felt like I was in the game, even as I wondered what hazard unbeknownst to me would pop up next.

I got my answer on the 427-yard, par-four fifth— the shortest par-four on the golf course. Most players were hitting a wedge for a second shot into a green that appeared different than the first four. There were grasses of two distinct colors on the surface: one a yellowish brown, the other a silvery steel green. I turned to

"The grass has adhesive qualities, so even though it's cut at the same height as the regular bentgrass, it only stimps at about five feet."

my host to inquire, but before I could verbalize the question he said, "Nearly twenty-five years ago, as green speeds approached twenty on the stimpmeter, the OWG approved Vika AB812 for use on the greens. The grass has adhesive qualities, so even though it's cut at the same height as the regular bentgrass, it only stimps at about five feet."

"So part of the green rolls at fifteen and other parts at five?" I asked in disbelief.

"That's correct," my host answered. "But you can see the difference in appearance from the landing zone in the fairway, so players plan their strategy for the second shot accordingly." Sure enough, I noticed that two of our group had left themselves in the channel of fast grass that approached the pin from the left side. My ball, on the other hand, had come to rest in a fast patch to the far right, with slow grass between me and another fast patch around the hole. This was bound to be an interesting putt.

Sensing where my ball was, where the cup was, and what percentage of which grass I needed to traverse, my scorecard had made some mathematical calculations and expressed the amount of inertia needed by my putter in an algebraic formula. It might as well have written it in hieroglyphics. I made what I thought was a reasonable stroke, and I watched it speed into the adhesive and skid to a stop. I still had several feet of AB (adhesive bent) to negotiate before it hit the slippery stuff again. Observers could easily have predicted the results of my next effort, as the ball raced past the flagstick and nearly off the green. As my host offered excuses for my putting naiveté, I slapped the ball twice more for your textbook four-putt.

The round was falling into a pattern—albeit not a very comforting one. Every time I felt a little more at ease with my rusty swing, another challenge I had never encountered reared up to intimidate me.

I was relieved when twenty-second-century technology helped me out on the seventh. I had driven into the woods to the left of the fairway, but my ball was easily found when it began to beep at the prompting of my scorecard. I never would have located it under the small plant that sheltered it, but once I did, the recovery shot back to the fairway was easily accomplished. That led to another bogey.

As we stood on the ninth tee, I was disturbed that I hadn't yet made one par. After my tee shot headed toward the lake on the right, it looked doubtful I'd break my streak on the last link on the outward half. The exact path my ball had taken was in question, as a hillside had obscured our view from the tee. When I asked our playing partners where I should drop, they referred me to the scorecard. "How should I proceed?" I asked, still feeling foolish talking to a piece of cardboard. "We need a ruling," came the reply.

Instantly, an image of a rules official, akin to holography from the 1990s, appeared in the fairway.

"Your ball entered the water hazard here, Mr. Grant," the official informed me, pointing to a spot on the embankment. "You can drop two club lengths from this spot in the tall grass, or anywhere back along the flight path, keeping the point of entry between you and the hole. Any questions?"

The instant I had regained control of my senses and managed a "No," the image disappeared. The entire incident took seconds, though I got the impression the apparition could go on endlessly citing chapter and verse of the rules, as well as the millions of decisions of precedence, should I require such. Take it in stride, I told myself.

The tenth hole was the most visually dramatic hole yet. A thin ribbon of fairway was embraced on both sides by sand stretching from tee to green. All of us found the beach with our tee balls, and Stillwater's came to rest close to mine. I guess I hadn't examined the bunkers on the front nine, because as we approached our balls I noticed the sand looked different than anything I had ever played from, although by now that was hardly a surprise. Sand was flashed up on nearly vertical walls in places; in other areas there were furrows six inches deep. One flat-looking expanse was punctuated by a series of holes with the sand in a vortex pattern spiraling downward to the bunker floor. The doctor filled me in as we walked.

"Sand particles are magnetized and can be made to adhere to any surface. A membrane below the bunker locks the placement and the charge is not diminished by rain, so the material can be made to hold any shape. This has eliminated washouts and drifting sand that would be common here on the Pacific Ocean. In fact, the original studies that led to magnetized sand were conducted right here at Bandon after years of unsuccessfully trying to keep sand in the bunkers during months of thirty-five-mile-per-hour winds.

"Course managers can also arrange the sand into any pattern they like—wavy ridges one day, checkerboard pattern the next, deep furrows for tournament days. If the variance is severe, you may have to play sideways back to the fairway rather than forward toward the green. That all started with trying to make bunker play more demanding than deep rough for professionals. Now it has trickled down to confound us hackers."

Sure enough, the sand in the part of the bunker we had arrived at was striped perpendicular to the direction of the hole. The height of the steps was about two inches, so whereas your ball on top might appear to be positioned for a clean shot, below the surface it had come to rest against one of the steps. Extricating myself from this predicament would obviously require a level of talent I didn't yet possess.

I chose a conservative play back to the fairway, sideways, taking my medicine and hoping to avoid the bunkers until I had a little more experience with them. Stillwater crushed his ball from a similar lie, though it returned to the sand three hundred yards ahead. When we arrived there we found the bunker in wavy ridges, so that his ball was resting in a valley between one-inch walls. As he blasted out to the green I noticed the magnetic charge kept most of the sand in the bunker with little infiltration to the putting surface—another plus for greenkeepers.

The seemingly endless walk and the mental fatigue from dealing with hazards I had never imagined began to take a toll on me over the last few holes. But my mood was buoyed on sixteen, an 861-yard par-five, where I made my first par. Driver, three-wood, and eight-iron put me on the putting surface—my second putt was not much more than a tap-in. I felt accomplished. "It usually plays into the wind," the doctor said, deflating my ego a tad.

The seventeenth was another shocker. From an elevated tee, an upthrust green erupted from a lake—one of those situations where you're either on the green or hitting again. The kicker was when my scorecard informed me the distance was only seventy-six yards. "Hitting it short is one of the toughest shots in golf these days," Stillwater said. "There are no tools to guarantee success, so you've got to finesse a wedge with a half swing."

Half swings were never one of my strong points, even on the best of days. So I addressed my ball with little confidence coursing through my mind. It showed. My first pass was a skull, my second a chunk. When I no longer cared, my third nearly went in. When all of us had hit, Stillwater instructed me to grab my golf bag and the hover devices whisked us away for a brief flight to the green. I tapped in for a six. I had just made a five on a 861-yard hole and a six on a 76-yard hole. Maybe golf hadn't changed all that much over the years.

The eighteenth green featured a different type of water hazard—ones that moved. Half-inch-deep waterways embraced the green, and you were expected to play from them should your ball come to rest there. Calm eddies in some spots held your ball's position. Currents in other places moved the ball away from the putting surface and into pools farther away. For the first time in the round, I had found the green with my approach shot, while my playing partners fell prey to the challenges. When they had all attained the putting surface in a sometimes hilarious display of splash shots, I lined up my thirty-footer. With no adhesive grass or sharp contours facing me, I ran the putt into the back of the cup for a birdie three. It was the kind of final hole that gives you reason to come back another day.

We retired to the grill room, where beer was still beer. The two I downed tasted better than anything I had experienced in my two weeks back on planet Earth. If you examined all the places I had been and all the things I had seen since I woke up at Western Wellness, the bar at Bandon Dunes was the most familiar sight. It bore a striking resemblance to the bars I had visited a century earlier. A slick bartender made small talk while he wiped down the counters; wait people picked up orders and delivered them to tables with baskets of pelletized bar snacks; a screen—albeit floating in midair—displayed a sporting event from elsewhere in the world; many of the same liquors were still lined up in front of the backing mirror; golfers kidded each other about their best and worst shots; women flirted; men boasted; employees loafed; and one guy leaned over the bar top and said in compromised English, "I'll just have one more before I go."

Chapter VI.

BACK AT THE DOCTOR'S residence, and having
now seen the face of golf in 2100, I immersed
myself in the literature of the game to gain context.
How and when did all the bizarre aspects of the
game come to be, and what was next in my twenty-
second-century golfing education?

I learned that golf had hit a low point midway
through the twenty-first century. Participation
waned; thousands of courses went out of business;
lucrative television contracts were canceled; only a
handful of equipment companies remained to swal-
low up the assets of the others; an entire generation
of kids shunned it; women left the game in record
numbers; and for a few years there was a good
chance golf would go the way of cricket or curling.

It was just as golf was teetering on the brink of extinction that the OWG was formed, bringing together all the remaining tours, networks, and associations from around the world. They added new forms of golf, spent untold millions of dollars to promote what they had, standardized equipment and rules, and rescued the game. In the process they tried to rewrite history by sweeping the problems under the rug, but it didn't work—the tarnished image took years to repolish.

I continued to find comfort and long-lost information in books. Outwardly, they looked exactly the same as they had a century earlier, though some of them featured interactive windows (akin to the scorecard) that made reading them a multimedia experience. This was especially handy for a book of a visual nature. Rather than look at a color photograph of a golf hole or course or hazard that had altered golf course evolution, any of those could now be displayed in three dimensions. And like the old golf simulators, you could put yourself on the eighteenth at the Old Course in St. Andrews—but the new simulation surrounded you and was so real it was hard to discern this virtual reality from the actual experience. I had given up trying to understand how such things worked.

I finally confronted Stillwater about his ability to answer my questions before I had asked them. The answer was about what I expected. "I can confirm your suspicions regarding my ability to read your mind," the doctor began. "As computer chip and medical technology evolved in tandem, it became possible to enhance the performance of every organ and every sense in the human body. The earliest implants merely monitored functions—heart rate, blood pressure, pulse, cholesterol levels, and the like.

"One of the advances that made computing faster and more compatible with human implantation was the conversion from slow silicon to rapid DNA as the building block of chip construction. The second generation of DNA chips allowed information to pass in both directions. Commands could be sent to various organs to perform in specific ways—produce more red blood cells; release antibodies to fight diseases; multiply the sensors in the nose for increased ability to smell; and even grow hair where it had stopped growing. The big leap was the interface of chips with brain development."

CHAPTER VI.

Stillwater gave pause, as if considering how much information I was able to understand. The way he spoke reminded me of how I spoke to my son when he was seven years old. "Remember how scientists once said we only used 10 percent of our brain? Well, today we believe that figure is closer to 35 percent. Among other things, the additional capacity has allowed us to project and detect thought patterns. That same thought that previously rattled around in your brain is now picked up by the chip and broadcast much like a radio wave. You can turn the thought off if it's something that shouldn't be shared, or you can enhance it when it's meant for public consumption."

"That same thought that previously rattled around in your brain is now picked up by the chip and broadcast much like a radio wave."

I was already taking inventory of all the thoughts I'd had while in the doctor's care.

He continued: "The receiving of brain waves is something that's cultivated by learning how to tune in to projections and by trading the first- and second-generation chips for models on the cutting edge of scientific development. Not everybody practices it. As a doctor I've had advanced training in tuning in to people's thoughts, and I possess the most highly tuned chip on the market. It makes me a better doctor diagnostically, especially with patients who are less than forthcoming."

Although this information was just what I had suspected, it left me uneasy. Was there no privacy? It was unsettling enough to know that Stillwater knew my thoughts; what about people with ill intent? "The reception of thoughts is an acquired skill," the doctor explained, "and one that is enhanced through cultivation. The person who hasn't practiced and developed his or her ability can pick up only the thoughts that are broadcast for mass consumption— kind of like junk mail or spam. This bombardment goes on constantly and is set at such a high frequency that most anyone can pick up on it, though a great deal of it is commercial in nature. Once you learn how to tune it in, the next trick is learning how to tune it out. Otherwise, as you progress through public places, it feels like every billboard is yelling your name and trying to get your attention.

"On the other side of the coin, projection can also be controlled or at least be selectively turned off and on through chip modification. The really advanced-thought people equipped with the latest technology can feel an inappropriate thought coming on and block its dispersal. Even people who have yet to cultivate the skill project their most deeply felt thoughts without even knowing it. The technology is still developing, and being a marriage of human development and computer advancement, the possibilities are limitless.

"I've got your parameters set so that only I can read your mind—something that has helped me both understand you and ease your entry into the modern world. I made the assumption that once you understood the technology involved you wouldn't be unhappy with me for setting the parameters as I have. Now that you understand the science, we can modify your settings in any way you want, and you can begin to cultivate the skills for your own good."

As I thought about that, Stillwater returned to our golf plans. "On a lighter note, the next step in your golfing education is X-Golf. Are you ready to move forward into that sphere?"

Rather than verbalize the answer, I tested the doctor's capacity by thinking an enthusiastic "Yes."

"Good," he said with a smile. "I've got some material for you to read, a match for you to watch, and a game set up for tomorrow. I'm a traditionalist myself, but X-Golf is far more popular than the traditional mode we enjoyed at Bandon Dunes. You'll be amazed." That seemed to be standard operating procedure these days.

Alternate golf games were nothing new, but these extremes were completely alien, yet necessary when the game's popularity started to slide. There were many factors: outrageous playing costs, glacial pace of play, decreasing interest in the etiquette and courtesy of the game, no landforms available for large-scale recreation, and society's preoccupation with violent sporting encounters—nearly all contributed toward spelling the end for such a staid and peaceful game. In some ways it was X-Golf that saved the sport from extinction.

Now with a seventy-five-year history of its own, X-Golf culminates in a World X-Game gathering once a year. Performance in a combination of several games results in the crowning of an individual and team champion, and the event is far more popular than national championships in traditional golf. The games include Speed Golf—a straight-out dead run for eighteen holes; Endurance Golf—about the same as Speed Golf, but play is extended to seventy-two holes; Altered Elements Golf (AEG)—where players adjust the environment to suit their game and complicate their opponent's; and Combat Golf—all-out war on the course, and the most popular variety.

Stillwater had scheduled us for a game of AEG the following day—although he was being strangely quiet regarding what that entailed. To keep me occupied he offered instructions on how to watch the finals of last year's Endurance Golf Championship, staged at the Royal Atlas Golf Palace in Morocco. To engage the program, all I had to do was think about viewing it; then I had the choice of scrolling it on my cornea, watching it as a projection on an "air screen," or being surrounded by it in simulator mode. I chose the latter, and suddenly I was part of the game. When I quickly realized I would have to run to stay abreast of the action, I returned to the room to view it as a projection in the comfort of an easy chair. It was strenuous enough just watching those supremely conditioned athletes speed by, never mind trying to keep up with them.

The four-course complex at Royal Atlas begins and ends in the Sahara Desert, but two of the layouts climb up into the foothills of the Atlas Mountains. On the desert floor the temperature often reaches 150 degrees (global climatic changes have ushered in a new era of extremes), and it is quite common to go without rain for years on end. When the burning wind blows hard from the south, it carries with it sand from the four million square miles of desert that lie below Royal Atlas. The sand feels like a sideways bombardment of thumbtacks coupled with a swarm of biting flies on any exposed skin; and the constantly shifting drifts affect contours of greens, depth of bunkers, and fairway conditions. In a severe blow, visibility is reduced to a scant few feet. It's easy to lose your bearings and end up wandering into uncharted territory. If you weren't being monitored via your chip implant, there's a good chance you'd never be found.

The Sahara, formed five thousand years ago, has been growing at an alarming rate in the past fifty years, slowly spreading its influence into higher and higher elevations. The poisonous snakes, badgers, and hyenas that occupy the outskirts of the desert are far from timid, and their interactions with golfers are legendary. Separated from the support network of course personnel, humans are just another species that these animals view with suspicion, disdain, and hunger. Golfers have learned not to turn their backs on a pack of them, and the scorecard states that you take your chances when you invade their habitat.

Temperatures cool quickly as the routing ascends into the hills, and gnarled trees begin to infiltrate the landscape. If a stiff wind is blowing at the upper elevations, the temperature variance can be as much as one hundred degrees from the desert floor—adding yet another complication to a taxing workout. The Atlas Mountain range includes three hundred peaks over nine thousand feet in elevation and six that tower beyond thirteen thousand feet. The hard-packed, red-brown earth is strewn with boulders. Occasionally, the barren hillsides are broken by high meadows covered with razor-sharp, wide-bladed grasses. The highest peaks are snow-covered year-round, and three-foot-tall snowbanks can even be found in sheltered areas at lower elevations in the middle of the summer. Within sight of the golf course are mud-and-rock Berber huts where native people live as they have for centuries. No mind projection or hovercrafts here—these inhabitants have never even experienced electricity or running water. They harvest their wheat

Temperatures cool quickly as the routing ascends into the hills, and gnarled trees begin to infiltrate the landscape. (Martin Grant illustration)

crop as they have for eons, and they view the intruders with curiosity and amazement.

Several facilities like this one, built in severe climates around the world in the last twenty-five years, serve as staging grounds for the World X-Golf Games. There are others in Siberia, Nepal, Brazil, and East Africa—and each provides challenge beyond the scope of the average player—even the average X-Game player.

At Royal Atlas, two of the courses measure over ten thousand yards. The other two are slightly shorter. Their cultivated areas are as fine as any layout in the world, but once you're off the fairways there isn't a hospitable square inch. Adding up the nearly forty thousand yards of golf and the distances between greens and tees, and the starting and ending points of the courses, players that hit it down the middle will cover nearly thirty miles—longer than marathon distance, every inch at an all-out running pace. The less talented will run even farther.

The finalists assembled for the world championship were the most finely tuned and ultimately conditioned athletes I had ever seen. All of them were nearly seven feet tall with perfect muscle tone and not an ounce of fat on their bodies. They would run a four-minute mile to warm up and not even break a sweat.

There is nothing about these specimens that isn't perfect, nor ever has been. From the moment of their conception—itself a scientifically arranged union between two breeders chosen for their physical and mental characteristics—their path has been ordained. Training begins in the womb with the host's chip implant directing muscle movement and dexterity enhancement. They can walk within hours of birth and run marathons in world-class times before they are three. Plasma synthesis, tissue fabrication, muscle-cell fortification, and organ-based repair circuitry are standard tools that leave no room for injury or weakness. The superathletes are cocooned from birth and develop no social skills, humor, or outside interests; athletic performance is their life. When their competitive careers are over at age thirty they must be retrained to join society. Many of them, unable to adjust, take their own life shortly thereafter. Despite entertaining the world during the height of their career, they die in obscurity, cast aside by a public that has little use for the aging sports star.

CHAPTER VI.

Innuew Pompé is the reigning men's champion—a sinewy twenty-three-year-old Brazilian with tawny skin and bright green eyes. A product of the South Amazon outpost, he has bulging elastic leg muscles, surgically implanted oversized lungs, leatherlike skin, and gigantic webbed feet. His pain receptors at every extremity of his body have been sealed. He plays barefoot no matter the conditions. He has won four World Endurance titles, his golfing strengths centered around his ability to run nonstop for days without the slightest increase in heart rate or breathing difficulty. On the course, he pauses for a second at the tee box and then launches the ball 450 yards down the middle of the fairway with astonishing regularity.

The number-one women's competitor is Sweden's Ulna Åndersshult. Stately and striking with platinum hair and black eyes, Åndersshult has dominated Endurance Golf for almost a decade, but a bevy of younger, stronger contenders feel this is the year to unseat her. She has used cunning and experience to stay on top, as well as a short game unmatched by any competitor. Sweden has been at the forefront of Enhanced Vision Technology (EVT) that allows the eyes to zero in like a telescope, charting and examining every inch of a ball's intended path in a split second. Åndersshult maps every nuance of the terrain as she runs to her ball; her interpolation enzymes convert the data to physical skeletal and muscle internode directives that control distance, direction, and force of the pitch shot. Her deadly accuracy has been tested in tournament conditions for years, and her statistics bear out the fact that she seldom fails. At age twenty-eight, her endurance is now in question and many wonder if she has reached the end of her domination of the sport. As the athletes gather, the world's attention turns to this display of muscle, stamina, touch, and tenacity.

Years of competition have proven that a great golfer who is a decent runner usually beats an average golfer who can run fast and hard. Hitting the ball long and straight saved time that could not be recovered otherwise, and the final score was always a combination of strokes played and time elapsed. The world record in Speed Golf for a 10,000-yard, 18-hole, par-72 course was 106:42, featuring one of the few sub-40-minute rounds ever recorded at 39:42, and a stunning score of five-under-par 67. (Combined, they equal the 106:42.)

CHAPTER VI.

No one could keep up such a pace in Endurance Golf. Even this super breed of athlete feels the fatigue. If the elements conspire against them, their golfing skills erode quickly, and every second counts. Many players have foozled their way to exhaustion after seeming vibrant when the rub of the green was going their way.

The public loved to see a titan tumble and thus expose their humanness, and these fans followed the game with fervor. They divided their loyalties equally between the speed runners and the superb golfers—hence the worldwide interest and heated arguments over who was better equipped to win. And team interests took precedence over the individual. More than fifty nations entered teams, some placing more than one, and the honor of world team champions was highly prized and deeply respected.

A team from Thailand was defending in the championship. They were being challenged by Sweden's best players and a new contender from New Zealand. Other strong teams from China, Peru, and the United States were in the running as well, and the complex leaderboard was perpetually changing to reflect a slowdown by one player or a high score by another. The lead changed hands several times every minute. It was clear that despite the fact the scores were cumulative for four golfers per team over the course of thirty miles of running and golf, the final standings would find the teams separated by just a few seconds. Likewise, the golf scores, which all had started under par and were now slowly working their way above, would be quite close.

Part of the challenge was steadying oneself for a four-foot putt after running for an hour at breakneck speed. Especially when the entire match might come down to a putt on the seventy-second green after more than two-and-a-half hours of exertion. A golfer from Thailand set the new individual world record at 449:36 (golf score of 280, running time of 169:36), breaking the 450 barrier for the first time. But Sweden, strong with great golfers who were good runners, won the title. I felt drained as the show ended, and wondered what the players did for fun. Golf had sure come a long way from Saturday morning at the club with the boys.

CHAPTER VII.

CHAOS IN THE ATMOSPHERE—ALTERED ELEMENTS GOLF—
ANXIETY CREEPS IN—TURNING UP THE HEAT—LET IT SNOW—
A RUB OF THE GREEN.

THE READING I HAD done during my slow days at the Stillwater residence had revealed another phase of life on Earth that had changed radically in the century since my former life—the massive alterations to the global climate. Many factors conspired to throw the planet's atmosphere into chaos—some triggered by society's actions, others that were naturally occurring.

It started with the amount of pollution and airborne particulates that were released from the industrial expansion. While the sophisticated nations did manage to slow the rate at which pollution entered the atmosphere, this was more than offset by the developing and Third World nations that felt few restrictions. Leaders from nations such as Korea,

Hungary, Gabon, Brazil, and China—economic powerhouses of the twenty-first century—were not fond of being preached to about environmental restrictions, especially when the admonishment came from governments they blamed for unchecked pollution in the previous century. The increase in carbon dioxide was astronomical, and the planet's temperature increased at an unparalleled pace. When a series of nuclear accidents released radiation into the mix, deadly cocktail clouds circled the globe at various altitudes, affecting entire climates when they were delivered to the surface by solar flares or massive storms.

If that wasn't enough, a decade of unprecedented volcanic activity midcentury exacerbated the problems. Massive eruptions in the western United States, Indonesia, Ecuador, and Iceland darkened the global skies and changed storm tracks, cooled the equatorial regions, defoliated the few remaining rain forests, and spawned tropical storms of greater fury than ever before experienced. Combined with the overall rise in global temperature that preceded it, especially apparent in the Polar Regions, the Earth's environment was in chaos.

CHAPTER VII.

The manifestation came in the form of a climate of extremes: an increase in excessively hot days, with corresponding spells of life-threatening cold. When the heat was polar-nested, glaciers melted, sea levels rose, and rainfall events were beyond comprehension. Rainstorms of twenty-five inches in a day were not uncommon—and when they hit sensitive ecologies the results were catastrophic. When yearlong cold spells shocked tropical regions, entire plant and animal species perished. Ancient, primitive societies vanished.

When the masses of polar heat collided with equatorial cold, hurricanes, typhoons, electrical storms, and tornadoes of tremendous fury were spawned. When these storms were infused with rogue clouds of radiation or toxic pollution, the effect was devastating.

The alteration of ocean circulation and the disruption of natural west-to-east progression of weather systems delivered severe weather to areas previously known for the gentle monotony of their climates. In 2071, the Mediterranean Sea froze after a yearlong winter with below-zero temperatures, accompanied by sixty feet of snowfall. Even scientists who felt they could fix *anything* realized that their efforts were futile.

The complacency of the early twenty-first century quickly vanished as it became clear that no amount of technology could correct the damage done to the Earth's climate. When meteorologists finally accepted the fact they had no chance to influence the weather—and, in fact, could barely predict it—efforts were channeled into preventing catastrophe. But the incubation period for extreme storms became shorter and shorter and the loss of life larger and larger. Even with the latest global monitoring equipment in place, deadly storms often took weather gurus by complete surprise.

Fortunately, force-field technology allowed some respite from the anger of Mother Nature. For nearly fifty years, environmental engineers had placed domes over ever-enlarging segments of the planet. Entire cities were now under invisible cover, so the procedure of enclosing a golf course was elemental. Many "outdoor" sports—including baseball, football, soccer, racing, and skiing—were now contested entirely "indoors." The semicircular force fields were clear, allowing natural sunlight to filter through, while repelling severe weather with the strength of a steel barrier. Inside the environment, wind and rain were easily created, either throughout the entire dome or at specific locales. Although I had read all about such innovations, I had yet to see them.

"Are you ready for AEG?" the doctor queried the next morning. "You realize that to fully explore the genre we must become adversaries, determined to do anything to win the match."

I knew what he was talking about and assured him of my determination. "I'm going to reduce you to a weeping mess; totally defeated by a 150-year-old neophyte," I boasted, throwing my chest out macho-style.

"Now you are becoming a man of the twenty-second century," Stillwater laughed. "Let's travel."

Altered Elements Golf was played on the sites of capped landfills, industrial waste properties, or former Superfund projects. Often the methane by-product of the landfill was captured and used to supplement solar and hydrogen sources in the enormous power requirements of the systems that support the facility. There are several in each region of the country, but it's enormously expensive to play at one, so demand is kept in check. Prices range into the tens of thousands of dollars for one round due to the technology involved, the resources needed, and the fact that only nine matches were allowed on the course at any one time. This spacing allows all the environmental adjustments to return to normal between groups.

The basic premise is simple. In a singles match the winner of the first hole is allowed to set the parameters of the next hole. If you make a birdie and your opponent can only manage a par, on the next hole you can adjust all the elements of the golf hole to your preference, and for your benefit. The array of available weapons is beyond what any twentieth-century golfer could imagine.

The victor could control the weather, as well as course conditions. Bring up the wind from a specific direction; make it rain, hail, or snow; increase or decrease the temperature; infuse the air with humidity to slightly decrease ball flight—these weather variables could be altered with merely a thought. Or punctuate the corridor of the hole with aerial hazards, raise the tilt and pitch of the green, and adjust the fairway to your liking—all done with ease. The routing of the course could not be changed—it featured an equal number of right and left doglegs, as well as a variety of short and long tests in every par.

I recalled seeing putting practice devices from the 1990s where the ten-foot-long carpeted runway could be adjusted by pistons underneath it to pitch the surface left or right in order to vary your challenges. This concept was now applied to five-hundred-yard-long fairways. Air-filled chambers running the length of the hole in the rough were part of the subsurface engineering, and they allowed the controlling golfer to quickly elevate the left and depress the right, and thus punish the slicer, or vice versa for the hooker.

There were other possibilities as well. You could elevate both sides of the rough, at which time the fairway becomes a collection zone with all errant shots funneled to the middle. That increased the excitement of low scoring. You could cant the first half of the hole severely right and the second half severely left, and that would bring out the rare shot-maker in the crowd. Or when both roughs were tilted to repel shots outward from the center line, the hogback fairway became nearly impossible to attain.

Once the player with the honor teed off, the hole could not be altered any further. Stillwater programmed the sensors to receive our thought commands between holes and wished me luck, and we stepped up to the first hole—a short, perfectly straight par-four devoid of hazards. "The first couple of holes are pretty plain," the doctor noted, "so as not to favor any one player's game. Until someone wins one we have no control over their parameters."

We both made bogey on the first, and I felt a certain anxiety creeping in as we moved to the second—another straight, though slightly longer par-four. The doctor made par on number two, and when my putt to match spun off the lip, I was not just one down in the match, I was also the PAM (player at mercy).

In the time it took us to walk to the next tee, the doctor's thoughts on how he wanted the hole set up had been translated into reality. Stillwater had depressed the mounding on the left so that a ball hit there would quickly cascade into the retention pond bordering the hole. With a slight increase in the elevation to the right side, he had enhanced his chances to keep his power fade in play, while decreasing the chances of my draw finding the short grass. I had expected this from the PIC (player in command).

I stroked a beautiful drive that started down the right side, curled into the fairway, and vigorously rolled toward the green; Stillwater's shot got hung up in the right side rough, defeating his intentions. I put my second on the green, while he found the deep bunker to the left. When he took two to escape the beach, I cozied my approach putt into tap-in range and won my first hole, squaring the match and grabbing the PIC position. The feeling of power was something I had never felt on a golf course before. It obviously radiated, judging from the smile that broadened on Stillwater's face.

The feeling of power was something I had never felt on a golf course before. It obviously radiated, judging from the smile that broadened on Stillwater's face.

"Feels pretty good to have control over the elements, doesn't it?" the doctor asked.

"It does, but I don't even know what to do with it yet," I countered as I mentally ran through my options on the way to the next tee box. It was an awesome feeling to be both golf course architect and Mother Nature. I settled on the obvious, merely reversing the fairway setup that my opponent had engaged. I waited until we reached the tee so I could watch the thoughts be transformed into reality—a process that happened with such speed that I could see why they wanted space between the matches.

"Those air-filled chambers beneath the fairways are much like the air bags in cars from your era," Dr. Stillwater said. "They fill—or deflate—with explosive power, and it takes only a second for the side of the fairway to change. Believe me, you don't want to be anywhere near there when the Earth starts to move."

Knowing I had bumpers along the left rough, I killed my tee shot. I watched it head toward that side and then quickly divert to the center of the fairway. Stillwater knocked one out of bounds and was forced to reload. I won the hole and took my first lead in the match as we approached the fifth tee.

Stillwater was still clobbering the ball up to fifty yards beyond my best stroke, so on the 824-yard, par-five fifth I engaged some aerial hazards to prevent him from using his length to unfair advantage. I placed the clouds 325 yards out, hoping to force him to lay up. But my carefully considered plan backfired. I hit first and really caught my tee ball— only to see it enter the nearest cloud and drop to the ground. Stillwater smirked as he launched a moonshot over all the hazards I had imagined, out-driving me by 150 yards. I still had 175 yards for my third shot, while Stillwater engineered a pitch-and-putt birdie to again even us up.

We had played only five holes, but the emotional roller-coaster ride was draining.

"Having fun?" the doctor quipped.

I had to admit I was. "This is terrific," I said. "It amplifies the old enjoyment of winning a hole a hundredfold. It's sure a great deal more fun than watching those guys in the Endurance Golf Championships. Here, every hole is an epic battle; it seems like we've been playing for days."

Stillwater said, "The AEG Championship is one of golf's most popular events, attracting such a large audience that it taxes the existing technology for viewing. The only thing that draws more people is Combat Golf, the difference being that we can play this form—I don't expect either of us will be participants in the other."

Our match settled down over the next several holes. We halved each until the ninth, where Stillwater brought the wind up. It was a crosswind that seemed to take relish in carrying my draw away from the fairway. It was blowing even stronger the farther down the hole we went—a fact he had failed to share with me. Although my tee ball stayed in play, my second shot drifted far to the left and landed in some nasty-looking rough. Escape was futile, and Stillwater closed out the front nine one up. He had also raised my ire more than any other time in the match. We walked between holes in silence.

He turned up the heat, literally, as we approached the tenth tee. "A little hot under the collar, Mr. Grant?" he laughed. "Try this on for size." Within seconds the sun was blazing, the air had been roasted dry, and the temperature had climbed to well over one hundred degrees.

He quickly hit and knocked one deep into the fairway. In the time it took for him to clear the tee and for me to get ready, the temperature had risen another ten degrees. My hands started to sweat, my throat burned, and my vision blurred. I tried to block it out as I swiped at the ball, focusing instead on my anger from the last hole. I hit my best drive of the day—maybe of the past hundred years.

The walk to our balls was arduous. My feet burned; the sweat had soaked through my clothing. A warm wind that smelled like fire came up. Our pace slowed even further. "Anybody ever die at one of these things?" I asked the attending physician.

"Don't forget that all your vitals are being monitored constantly," Stillwater replied. "If anyone gets critical there's a medical team on the course in a minute." He hesitated. "But of course accidents do happen," he said with a devilish grin. We tied the tenth hole, but quite frankly, I can't remember much about it. I was lost in a heat haze until we climbed onto the eleventh tee, where it was seventy degrees with a light breeze. We both drank readily from the water supply and regained our strength.

The eleventh seemed straightforward until we approached the green. Stillwater had tilted it severely, and being below the hole was paramount. I wasn't, he was: two down with seven to play.

The twelfth was the course's short hole—only eighty-seven yards to a volcano green, surrounded by water. Stillwater bowled the green, hoping he could prevent one of his long balls from hitting the surface and bouncing off into the abyss. It was no use. After he dunked two in the water well beyond the back of the green, I nipped a half wedge to fifteen feet. He conceded the putt as he grumbled while walking off to the thirteenth. "You'll have to teach me that shot sometime, Grant," he muttered. It made me chuckle to think that a man who could power the driver 450 yards down the fairway didn't have a chance inside 100 yards.

I waited to see the next hole before making any decisions on its disposition. Good decision. It reminded me of the eighteenth at Pebble Beach: a gentle left hard curl along a water hazard of about 525 yards. For 2100, that was nothing more than a short par-four, but I felt we needed some classic Pebble Beach weather to complete the picture. Slowly, the wind rose off the water and it began to rain; a sprinkle while we were teeing off that built into a sideways pelting by the time we reached our shots. It was blowing a gale greenside and Stillwater knew he'd have trouble holding the ball against it.

"Too bad you never played at Pebble Beach," I shouted at the tall man who was having difficulty standing up straight. "We played in weather like this every winter." Stillwater apparently didn't feel my comments warranted a reply and went about the business of his preshot routine. I could see him trying hard to concentrate, but his off-balance swing was sloppy. His ball rifled into some fescue right and short of the hole. When he eventually reached the putting surface, I had the luxury of three putts for the win. Once again we were even.

It was easy to see why this particular game of golf attracted people. Golf has always required an advanced skill set with tools ranging from an empty brain and a keen eye to big shoulder muscles and a jeweler's touch. One outing might require the perseverance and patience of a saint; the next round the power and glory of a soldier. In one round of AEG every emotion, every need, every bit of cunning, every ounce of creativity, and every speck of skill was required. It was hard to be passive or detached—the action was far too compelling. I can't imagine people being able to handle playing it on a regular basis.

I decided to press my luck as we arrived at the fourteenth—a 307-yard par-three. The rain slowly changed to fluffy snow, and the temperature dropped into the forties. I wondered if Stillwater had even been in the snow before. "Are you kidding, I ski in the Rockies every winter," he bellowed. "Plus, I came prepared for just such a ruse." He pulled hand warmers from his bag and played away, blasting his two-iron toward the green.

The rain slowly changed to fluffy snow, and the temperature dropped into the forties. . . . He pulled hand warmers from his bag and played away, blasting his two-iron toward the green.

It was another backfired endeavor, and Stillwater made me pay. He flaunted his warm hands as the air chilled and snow stuck to the ground. He found the green from the tee, while my ball snuggled into a little hollow to the front left. If I hadn't played it quickly, we might have lost it in a snow drift. The deft touch I needed had frozen up, and his two-putt par was a winner. It was a familiar golfing story. Every time I drew close and felt some confidence, my opponent slapped me down and grabbed the lead.

I knew the green looked oddly familiar as we stood over our second shots on fifteen, but I wasn't sharp enough to recognize a striping pattern of fast and sticky grass. The doctor's ball came to rest in a fast avenue with a direct path toward the flagstick, while I had to cross four different stripes to reach the hole from where I was. You really have to rock the pill to get it through ten feet of molasses, an unnatural act when the slick portions run faster than polished marble. I left my first putt twenty feet short, but ran my second thirty feet past. I eventually tallied as many putts as Stillwater had strokes on the hole, and I found myself two down with three to play.

Bear down, I pep-talked myself. This is no different than a match with the guys back in Monterey. Expect the unexpected and go about your business. Don't use the weather or course conditions as an excuse—just swing the club through the ball and accept your fate.

Great soliloquy—until I stepped onto the sixteenth tee and discovered that my opponent had ordered up a fifty-mile-per-hour tailwind. Stillwater knew the 587-yard par-four quite well. Even though we couldn't see the conclusion from the tee, he thought he could drive the green with that howler at his back. His "normal" 425-yard drive took off into the void—headed directly at the green as it disappeared from our view.

I refused to be intimidated. I grabbed a four-iron and made a relaxed pass at the ball. My shot split the fairway and rode the wind for 310 yards. We arrived at my ball still not knowing what had become of the doctor's. The wind was blowing so strong at my back that sand grains escaping the bunkers felt like pushpins to the skin. I could probably have hit seven-iron the remaining 270 yards. Instead, I grabbed my two-iron and hit a shot I had relied on during a visit to Scotland. Ball back in the stance, flat three-quarter swing, pick a spot a hundred yards out, and try to roll the ball over it.

The execution was textbook. The ball never reached ten feet in elevation, but it shot toward the green like a Yogi Berra line drive. You could have read the front page of the paper while it scampered, bumped, scooted, and rolled toward the putting surface, eventually climbing onto the open front and elegantly running out of steam four feet below the hole. Even my opponent stopped to applaud.

Stillwater's ball had cleared the green in the air and found a home in some of the deepest rough on the course, down an embankment with overhanging trees hampering a recovery. He played a marvelous shot to find a corner of the green, and two putts later he was in for an accomplished par. But I was not going to let it divert me from my focus. I paused for a moment, thought what I was doing, and nailed my birdie into the back of the cup. I felt like Tom

CHAPTER VII.

Watson at the British Open in the 1970s as I strode to the seventeenth, now just one down.

The second-to-the-last hole was striking: a narrow ribbon of elevated, rough-less fairway surrounded by oceans of sand. I decided that subtlety might be my best bet on such a garish stage, and opted for a trio of alterations. I ordered a light left-to-right breeze, barely noticeable on the tee. I tilted the fairway in the drive zone ever so slightly to the right. And I willed deeply furrowed sand patterns just about where Stillwater's drive might come to rest. The doctor watched my safe four-wood come to rest on a firm piece of real estate, and I could tell he was wondering what I had up my sleeve.

He made a tired swing that he failed to finish. The ball caught the outskirts of the fairway but bounded and rolled until it hopped into the sand and disappeared.

The hole was short and my nine-iron competent enough to offer a birdie opportunity. His ball sat in a sand channel with walls that extended above the height of the ball. The required explosion shot could not advance the ball far enough to find the dance floor, and the doc's touch was not up to snuff

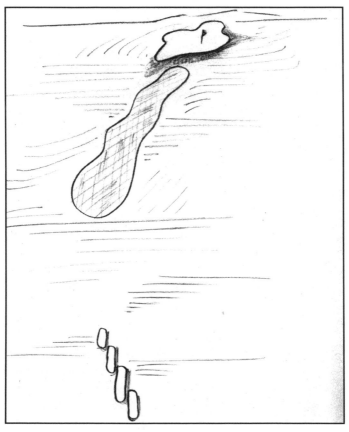

The second-to-the-last hole was striking: a narrow ribbon of elevated, rough-less fairway surrounded by oceans of sand. (Martin Grant illustration)

when he played his third. I won the hole with a par four, and our battle was all square as we came to the home hole. I couldn't believe how much fun this had been—but I was determined to keep the game face on for another fifteen minutes.

The eighteenth was a difficult uphill par-four with fortified bunkers to the right of the drive zone and a pond to the left of the green. I hesitated to make massive changes because I had already seen the radical alterations backfire on more than one occasion. My opponent eyed me suspiciously as he scanned for changes. I acted mysteriously and kept quiet, figuring the absence of the outrageous might throw him off more than the anticipated. We both stroked sound drives and walked in silence to our balls, which were separated by a scant ten yards.

For the first time all day I had outdriven Stillwater. He had hit a three-quarter three-wood in order to avoid the fairway bunkers, while I had tagged my driver. I could feel him trying to read my thoughts regarding what challenges I had concocted greenside, but I blocked his inquiry and prodded him to play away. His swing was tentative. Even though the ball's flight looked good, the shot was slightly short. It was siphoned off the front of the green into thick rough, while I tried not to get too excited.

I pulled my six-iron ever so slightly and watched nervously as it fell to earth, landing in the rough dangerously close to the water boundary. Given my normal ball flight, nine times out of ten it would have taken an accelerating right-to-left kick and splashed into the drink. But this was the odds breaker. The ball hopped straight up instead of left, made a second smaller hop back toward the green, found the edge of the putting surface, and slowly started trickling in the direction of the hole. When it died it was only five feet away from the cup.

"What the hell happened to that?" Stillwater screamed.

"Just the rub of the green, I guess," I said as if nothing unusual had occurred. Stillwater was rattled and his stubbed pitch showed it. When it was my turn to play I capitalized on that stroke of good fortune and drilled the ball into the back of the hole, winning the match. It was one of the greatest feelings I had ever enjoyed.

CHAPTER VIII.

LAWYERS IN 2100—COMBAT GOLF—SOME THINGS
NEVER CHANGE—BLOOD AND BONE-JARRING
COLLISIONS—BOX SEATS.

O UR FLIGHT BACK TO Stillwater's was mostly in silence—not because we were still adversaries, but because of the overwhelming nature of the experience. As compelling as the other forms of golf had been, Altered Environment Golf really separated itself.

"Is everyone so awed by their first AEG experience?" I asked the doctor.

"It is compelling no matter how many times you've played," he said. "And many people never get a chance to play at all. Pricing and availability make it difficult for most people to enjoy it. One round is equal to several months' salary for the average Joe, and the few facilities in the country are booked for months in advance. It is more of an amusement for the well-to-do than anything."

93

I mulled that over while my host added, "But the answer to your original question is, yes. Being able to control the playing field and the forces of nature has few parallels in other athletic contests. It gives people a feeling of power they don't realize in many other endeavors whether connected to sport or not. AEG has only been around for fifteen years or so, and as the technology advances the cost may come down, so it could become a more common pursuit in the future."

In the following days I began to think about my own future. I couldn't live with Stillwater forever, but I had no home, no skills, no money, and no job. I started to work on developing personal thought projection and detection. I wasn't sure if it was possible for someone with a 150-year-old brain to cultivate such development, but I was determined to try. I had modest success and as the "junk mail" of thought projection reached my mind I was initially thrilled. Then I learned that tuning it out was a needed skill that went hand-in-hand with tuning it in. That was even harder. I did make progress and could even tune in to Stillwater if he "shouted" his thought projection at me.

I wondered about the role of lawyers in 2100. Without mastery of the latest technology or the ability to read thoughts, I would surely be at a disadvantage to my peers—especially in court. Never mind digesting the thousands of decisions that current law was based on. How many times in my previous career had I cited legal opinions that were a hundred years old? Not many—and it was probably fewer today. Stillwater jolted me out of the depression I was courting when he announced we'd be attending two golfing events of note the following day.

"It's time you see just how far golf has fallen in some circles," Stillwater laughed. "We'll stop by the Western Regional Combat Golf Championships and watch some of the best teams in the country trying to annihilate each other. If you thought AEG was vindictive and nasty, you're in for another shocker."

I was getting used to shockers. I was even expecting them at this point.

"I have arranged for us this afternoon to attend the third round of the United States Championship of the Order of World Golf—what used to be the U.S. Open in your era. It's being held at Bethpage State Park in New York, so you'll get your first look at the East Coast and an older course. That's one of the few where they had the room to push the tees back a couple of thousand yards to keep it challenging for the professionals."

Given the gap I had always known between my play and the touring pro's abilities, I could scarcely imagine how far they hit or what an arsenal of tricks was up their sleeves. We always thought that no one could be better than Jack Nicklaus—then Tiger Woods—but today, I bet they'd look like Old Tom Morris did to us in our day.

The following dawn brought bright sunshine and warm temperatures. Stillwater warned me, however, that Combat Golf was played outside without force-field shields no matter what the weather conditions, so I should be prepared. We flew in about an hour before game time, and the site was quite a spectacle. Giant bleachers—which held the largest crowd I had seen assembled in one place since my awakening—were at the center of a six-hole course that looped around them. By turning and twisting you could see play on every hole, and, of course, there were giant video displays and hand-held personal terminals if you had trouble locating the players.

The spectators were boisterous and active: chanting, yelling, drinking, fighting, and demonstrating for each other. *Some things never change*, I observed. As the teams sped into the arena the stands erupted. Instead of the hover donut being around the golf bag, as it had when Stillwater and I played, it was now tightly fitted around the golfer, allowing a full swing before rocketing after the ball at nearly the same velocity. As they began to warm up it reminded me more of Roller Derby in the 1970s than golf in 2000.

Stillwater tried to fill me in on protocol above the din of the masses. "There are three players per team on the course at all times—a driver, an iron player, and a putter. The driver tees off and, hopefully, sends it in the direction of the fairway player. As soon as it comes to rest, he can smack it toward the green. The putter can putt it, but if short game shots or bunker play is needed, anyone from the team can join in at any time—although, still, the ball must come to rest between all shots. The ultimate object is to get the ball into the hole, move on to the next hole, and complete three loops of the six-hole course. The score doesn't matter, only the time in which you complete the course."

Seemed pretty easy, but I knew they called it Combat Golf for some reason. "The difficulty lies in the fact that there are two other teams trying to do the same thing at the same time. And there are few rules; virtually anything goes. You can substitute for downed players, but there's a limit to how many team members are active for a game. And injuries are common—violence is, in fact, encouraged. Putting these kids back together again after one of these big matches challenges our best medical technicians."

I could tell this wasn't the doctor's favorite pastime, and a look at the crowd revealed few other professionals. This was the same gang that went to stock-car racing in my day.

We were sitting close to the action, giving me a good look at the players as they assembled prior to tee off. These kids were young teenagers and looked like frustrated hockey players or tag-team wrestlers on pay-per-view. They came from combat golf clubs all over the West, where local leagues were active year-round. This particular match featured teams from Montana, Seattle, and Scottsdale. It was really hard to believe this is what golf had come to.

With little fanfare, three strapping young men assumed their positions at the broad first tee, while their counterparts flew to the other assigned stations on the first hole. There was a moment of silence and then the crowd and the players exploded like the opening of the gates at the Kentucky Derby. Balls, people, and clubs were flying everywhere, and the fans loved it.

One team jumped out to an early lead, while the other two battled in the first fairway. A Seattle player was knocked in the side of the head by a high-velocity iron shot—his team retaliated by blind-siding a Scottsdale offender just as he was about to chip. He went sprawling into some rocks, and when he didn't get up immediately, a replacement flew in.

The Montana team was slowed by some errant shots. When they were caught by Seattle there was hell to pay. A player was clothes-lined as he flew to a ball, while another was flattened face-first into a bunker just after making impact with a ball. Blood, flying body parts, and bone-jarring collisions brought waves of loud approval from the stands as patrons got into the spirit of the battle.

The six-hole loop could be negotiated in well under ten minutes, even with combatants trying to kill each other, so each match lasted less than a half-hour. The tournament was double elimination and play went on all day—we stayed about an hour and watched two matches. I'd seen enough after a few minutes to know that, had they been here, nine-teenth-century golf traditionalists would have been reaching for the hemlock.

Our flight time across country was about an hour and a half. Stillwater had brought his larger and more powerful hovercraft, approved for long-range travel on this trip. Its comfort and extra space was appreciated. As we traveled, he filled me in on what had become of the U.S. Open.

"For fifty years, people discussed limiting the flight of the golf ball, but, believe it or not, no one had the guts to do it. During that time the number of high-quality courses that could host a major championship slowly was reduced to just a few venues. Finally, after those monstrous courses had been

Stillwater had brought his larger and more powerful hovercraft, approved for long-range travel on this trip. Its comfort and extra space was appreciated. (Martin Grant illustration)

"Pros could hit it five hundred yards and putt with uncanny accuracy. Winning scores went down every year for decades. The public became jaded to such monotonous excellence."

pushed out to their extremities and the governing bodies had used all the weapons available to protect par, a standard ball was approved for the world's major championships. Along the way, spectators lost interest. Pros could hit it five hundred yards and putt with uncanny accuracy. Winning scores went down every year for decades. The public became jaded to such monotonous excellence. Traditional golf championships didn't have the spark or fire of the X-Golf games," Stillwater said with a certain remorse.

"To make matters worse, the decade of the 2060s was filled with assassinations, some of famous sports figures and often on live broadcasts being seen by millions of people. The governing bodies were forced into some kind of reaction. So they severely restricted access to the sites—not just in golf but other sports as well. Some of the marquee players refused to participate unless such steps were taken.

"As virtual technology improved, spectators could 'feel' the games right from their homes anyway, so the backlash wasn't as severe as you might expect.

CHAPTER VIII.

However, for at least ten years, only the media and rules officials could attend golf championships. Now they are relaxing the restrictions slightly. Currently, a limit of a thousand spectators are allowed on the premises, and those people are subjected to extensive background checks and complete screening and inspection before they enter."

Stillwater had pulled some strings to get us in, though I could tell it was as much for his benefit as mine. "I haven't been to an Open since I was a kid, and I saw Tiger Woods play in his last major."

"You saw Tiger play?" This seemed impossible given the fact I had seen Tiger play a century ago.

"He retired and entered politics when he was fifty, and played in his last U.S. Open in 2026. I was eight years old."

I quickly did the math and did it again when the answer didn't make sense.

"You're eighty-two?!" I blurted in utter disbelief.

"Correct," Stillwater said. "Why does that surprise you?"

"I had thought sixty, but I guess I was using twentieth-century yardsticks." I scarcely had the time to process the fact that an eighty-two-year-old man could hit the golf ball more than four hundred yards before we approached Bethpage. The complex, down to three courses in order to provide enough room for one world-class test of golf, was gleaming green in a sea of concrete, steel, and glass. The New York City borders had pushed out into Long Island, but Bethpage had held its ground. This week it hosted the world's best players.

I asked the doctor if any of Tiger's records were still intact. "Tiger broke every record that Jack Nicklaus set," Stillwater said. "But then all those records were broken by Ingswen Kååtsen of Finland half a century later. Now Kååtsen's records are being threatened by Kamlapati Samir of Calcutta, India. He's a machine—technically perfect on the golf swing—as well as a spirit, living in a meditative state that allows him to shut down and draw power from his inner being between shots. He turned professional at age thirteen and in seven years has won dozens of world championships. He's the defending champion today."

We entered a skybox to follow the action. The small room had limited hover capabilities, allowing you to move about the course a hundred feet or so above the action. Screens inside the unit projected the progress of many different groups, and you could program another camera from the box to follow any action you wanted. Fortunately, the boxes were completely silent because there were several hundred of them hovering about the property. You had to keep an eye out for where you were going.

"You know how golfers sold advertising space on their bag, hat, or shirt in your era?" Stillwater asked. "Well, these days they sell their thoughts. For a fee, any fan can get inside the mind of Samir as he comes down the stretch and hear exactly what his thought process is. Should he lay up on the par-five or go for it? Does he draw a six-iron or fade a seven on the par-three? What line is he looking at as he lines up his putt? Answers to these and much more are available right then and there, not in some post-round interview when the facts may change due to the outcome. People pay good money for that insight."

Samir was on fire while we watched; knocking irons stiff from three hundred yards out and making birdies. Stillwater had paid for our access to his thoughts, but my skills weren't developed enough to get everything. At one point, as he hit an approach to a par-four, I did catch the swing thoughts of the best player in the world just before he launched. He was repeating over and over, "Swing easy and keep your head down." Some things never change.

CHAPTER IX.

PLANS FOR A PILGRIMAGE—MY SON?!—SIR TOBIAS
MAITLAND-BRICKENDALE—HICKORY CLUBS AND GUTTIES—
SMILES ALL AROUND.

O N THE WAY HOME I had to admit that the Open was the least compelling of the golf events we had watched over the course of the past month. It seemed clear to me that people who thought inflicting bodily harm was part of golf would have little interest in speaking in hushed tones, waiting for one more endless preshot routine to conclude in yet another near-perfect shot. Boring.

Stillwater broke a long, thoughtful silence: "Your golfing education is nearly complete; there's just one more place I think you should see."

"I don't know how you can top what you've shown me so far," I replied, ready for yet another bizarre futuristic ritual.

"We need to make a pilgrimage to St. Andrews in Scotland. There are some things going on there you'd be interested in. I'll see if I can set it up for next week."

The thought of visiting St. Andrews filled my head for the rest of the ride home. I had been there in the 1970s as a twenty-year-old, and I had played virtual golf there when I first arrived at Stillwater's, but I could not imagine what it had become in light of the rest of the world of golf.

In the next few days we discussed submitting my story to the Planetary Information Network and bracing for the invasion of my privacy that would entail. Stillwater also widened his search for any relatives of mine, and the work finally paid dividends.

"I have located a relative of yours," the doctor greeted me one morning.

I pictured some great-grandchild I would have never met—one who had heard the long-ago tale of the old man who was swallowed by the great earthquake.

"It's your son," Stillwater announced.

Given the human longevity of this era, my mind had toyed with the idea that people I knew might still be alive, but this was still a mind-blower.

"He's 115 years old," I said, stating the obvious.

"That's right," the doctor said, "and from what I've heard, still in quite good shape. He lives in a senior city in Oklahoma. I figured you might want to make contact with him before we go public."

Everything I had done so far in 2100 had been weird, but this would top the bill. I was elated, yet the excitement was mixed with anxiety and trepidation. I had to settle into the idea before I moved forward, and I wondered if I should give him the same opportunity by calling before I showed up at his doorstep. It seemed the right thing to do, but the thought of a surprise visit was also precious. We decided to hold off on that endeavor and breaking my story to the rest of the planet until after the trip to Scotland.

Stillwater wouldn't clue me in to what was going on at St. Andrews, but he was sure it would catch my fancy. Transoceanic flights were not recommended for personal hovercraft, so we boarded a commercial flight. The transporter resembled the Space Shuttle from a hundred years ago, though it took off like an airplane and was propelled by rockets as it hurtled along the runway. We climbed rapidly until we were on the edge of the Earth's atmosphere and able to make extraordinary time. Less than two hours later we touched down in London, where we caught a high-speed train to a stop just a few hundred yards from the first tee at the Old Course. It had only been two hours and twenty-eight minutes from when we departed from the airport in California.

"There isn't a place on the planet that takes more than four hours to get to," Stillwater informed me.

I voiced concern about our golf clubs, to which the doctor replied, "You won't need them." Now he had really raised my curiosity.

We were ushered into the clubhouse of the Royal and Ancient Golf Club amidst an air of clandestine secrecy—somehow appropriate for an institution that had guarded its position in the world of golf since 1754. Stillwater knew the current captain of the R&A: Sir Tobias Maitland-Brickendale, a former physician who had served on a world health advisory board with my host. As we were escorted down dark hallways, decorated with archaic paintings and dusty memorabilia, I wondered how much had changed in the past century at the R&A—if anything had at all.

"Hey, Brick," Stillwater greeted his ancient friend. "How's life treating you?"

I saw the frail and pale shadow of a man who could barely stand, even with the aid of a cane. He was one of the few people I had seen in 2100 who was shorter than I was, and he seemed to need the doorway of his office as support. "Gettin' by, for a hundred-year-old," Brickendale answered with a slight smile. "And yourself, my dear doctor?"

I was introduced, and the two then exchanged pleasantries while I looked about the room. It was the first time I had seen much paper in my travels— Brickendale's desk and conference table were stacked high with memos, letters, papers, folders, and stuff—it reminded me of my own office in the 1980s, before computers began to tidy things up. It was hard to believe this office was the command post for an organization that still held considerable power in the Order of World Golf (OWG).

"Excuse the mess, but I'm preparing for my presentation to the Links Trust next week. As you know, we're trying to get Edict 714 passed, and I expect a fight," Brickendale said, a sparkle in his eyes. Stillwater asked his friend to background me, claiming I had been out of golf for a number of decades.

"Well, as you probably know, seventy-five years ago there was nothing more we could do to protect the integrity of the game on the Old Course. The tees had been pushed back as far as the land allowed, the bunkers deepened, the greens sped up far beyond what the architect intended. Amateurs were driving par-fours and shooting in the low 60s with regularity. The Trust refused to integrate the new generation of hazards that are so prevalent everywhere else into the mix, and slowly the course became a shadow of its former self. That's when we instituted one heritage day a week."

The tees had been pushed back as far as the land allowed, the bunkers deepened, the greens sped up far beyond what the architect intended. Amateurs were driving par-fours and shooting in the low 60s with regularity.

I acted like I knew what a heritage day was, for fear of appearing like a dolt if I didn't.

"We're now up to four heritage days out of six, but the traditionalists want every playable day," Brickendale added. "Of course, the layout will always remain closed on Sundays, per Old Tom's wishes."

It was wonderful to hear of a reverence for the past—tradition was not something that seemed valued in the 2100 world.

"Is there enough material to supply that sort of demand?" Stillwater asked.

"Our forest is at full maturity, and the renewal plan seems to keep pace with increased needs, so I don't foresee a problem in that regard," Brickendale noted. "Have you shown Mr. Grant the operation?"

Stillwater said we were on our way there now, but he had wanted to introduce me to Brickendale first. We said our good-byes and wandered back out to the street. The streets around St. Andrews looked strikingly similar to my recollection from 130 years ago. But when we strolled into Auchterlonie's Golf Shop, I realized things had changed—St. Andrews had gone back in time.

The shop was filled with young men making golf clubs and balls: the clubs from hickory; the golf balls from gutta percha.

Said the doctor: "The Links Trust maintains a forest in the Scottish Highlands, where they planted hickory trees for clubmaking and Malaysian sapodilla trees for gutta percha. As they harvest, they replant, and the raw materials are brought here. Using the original techniques, these craftsmen make hickory clubs and gutties. If Brickendale's followers have their way, eventually that's the only equipment with which you'll be allowed to play the Old Course."

Stillwater had surprised me again, but this time with a scenario from 1850—not 2100. Our round with the ancient weapons was delicious—featuring 185-yard drives, spoons from the fairway, and making due from the bunkers. Nothing remotely like a sand wedge existed to extricate balls from the cavernous pits that dotted the landscape. We scrambled, played along the ground to stay out of the wind, crafted cunning half shots, fashioned bump and runs—the whole nine yards. Others on the course were dressed in traditional garb that included plus-fours and white shirts with little black ties. There were no electronics, nothing hovered, and the greens stimped around eight so you really had to whack it.

Stillwater tried to learn shots he had jealously watched me play. I could tell that with a little practice even he could become a golfer of the nineteenth century. Our contest came down to the eighteenth green where he hopped the stymie I had laid him and beat me one up. I think the smile stayed on both our faces all the way home.

Epilogue.

PAUL—SENIOR GOLF—ONE OF THOSE PERFECT DAYS (AGAIN).

STILLWATER HAD ARRANGED A meeting with my son Paul at his doctor's office. After Paul's normal checkup, Stillwater was introduced as a consulting physician who had an unusual matter to discuss with him. He probably thought he had some incurable disease as the doctor talked of cryogenics and human longevity, but watching through a one-way mirror I could tell Paul was suspicious. When I walked through the door, the recognition was instant. We both began to weep as we embraced.

I could still see the fifteen-year-old I had left behind in his face, and he had always remembered what I looked like—it's not easy to lose your father when you're a teenager. But now the child I had known as an infant and had lost when he was still in

115

high school was an ancient man, and I was sixty-five years younger than him. Even though I had much longer to prepare for such an event, neither of us could believe it.

We spent two days catching up on the past hundred years. He relived the pain of my accident and the aftermath of not getting to share the accomplishments of his youth. We talked about my wife who had lived more than fifty years beyond my life's interruption. We covered his career as an attorney and then a judge and how the profession had changed. (He even offered that he might be able to pull a few strings and get me a job—now there's a turnaround.)

We looked at photos of his kids, grandchildren, and great-grandchildren, and he detailed their lives. We spoke of his retirement and the pleasures of living in the new senior cities that had been developed. Like all parents, I was pleased to know he had enjoyed a good life and amazed that I would once again be a part of it. The encore was sweeter than the performance, even if we only had a limited time on stage together.

Eventually, Paul turned to me, and in a voice so similar to one I had locked away in the precious memory section of my brain, said, "Can we go out and play some golf, Dad?"

Senior golf was a hoot. Holes were short; hazards were few. All roads led to the flagstick as fairways were embanked to keep the ball near the center stripe. Greens were pitched to help shots find the cup. At age 115, Paul could still hit the ball about two hundred yards—roughly the same distance he could hit it when I last played with him in the year 2000. We laughed at that and had a grand old time on the nine-hole links right outside his doorstep.

As we walked off the final green, Paul turned to me and said, "You know, I still have something here in my golf bag that you may remember." He pulled a wrinkled yellow scorecard from a pocket and offered it to me. "I found this in the mass of twisted metal that was once your car. It's your scorecard from that round at Pebble Beach you played the day of your accident. I've relied on it for inspiration many times in the past century."

I fondled the piece of cardboard and opened it slowly. There was the three penned in to the eighteenth hole and circled, and just beyond it the total score of 76. The signatures of my playing partners were still visible, and I was immediately transported back to that wonderful experience, even though it really didn't seem that long ago to me. I got goose bumps just thinking about it, and tears came to my eyes once again—something that had happened many times in the precious days I spent with Paul. "Tell me about that round, Dad," my son said to me.

"Well, it was one of those perfect days—the kind that come around once or twice each golfing season . . ."